9-96

Sally Arnold

Sally Arnold

CHERYL RYAN

Illustrated by

BILL FARNSWORTH

COBBLEHILL BOOKS/DUTTON
New York

Library of Congress Cataloging-in-Publication Data
Ryan, Cheryl.
Sally Arnold / Cheryl Ryan;
illustrated by Bill Farnsworth.
p.   cm.
Summary: A lonely girl befriends an elderly woman
who collects things.
ISBN 0-525-65176-4
[1. Loneliness—Fiction.   2. Friendship—Fiction.
3. Old age—Fiction.   4. Country life—Fiction.]
I. Farnsworth, Bill, ill.   II. Title.
PZ7.R948Sal 1996 [E]—dc20 94-6455 CIP AC

Published in the United States by Cobblehill Books,
an affiliate of Dutton Children's Books,
a division of Penguin Books USA Inc.,
375 Hudson Street, New York, New York 10014

Designed by Kathleen Westray
Printed in Hong Kong

First Edition   10 9 8 7 6 5 4 3 2 1

For Marc and Sarah
and all who have ever gone down
Sally's Backbone to Fox's store.
C.R.

To my daughter Allison.
B. F.

J enny Fox was bored. She had already swept the floor,
arranged the canned goods, and sampled the candy just
to make sure it was still sweet. All this and it was still only
Monday. She was glad she had come to stay with Grandpa
this summer, but she missed her friends back in town. Jenny
wished she could make some new friends here.

Grandpa only pretended to need her help in his general
store. Most of his customers came on Saturday night. They
would buy what they needed for the week and visit with
their country neighbors at the same time.

Jenny got out her fiddle. Played lively dancing tunes. Pretended it was Saturday night and the store was full of smiling, dancing people. Jenny wandered over to the big front windows. She put down her fiddle and stared. Sally Arnold walked by.

"What a scary-looking woman," Jenny thought. "She looks like a witch in a fairy tale." Jenny had heard customers tell of Sally Arnold. How she lived by herself. How her shack at the end of the hollow looked ready to slide into the creek. How wherever she went, old Sally never went empty-handed. How she was always collecting things to make into something.

Since coming to the country, Jenny had seen Sally searching the ditches and road banks, nearly hidden by weeds.

"Searching for berries, mushrooms, or wild asparagus," Grandpa had told Jenny. Sometimes the old woman brought him ginseng and old bottles or one of her gathering baskets for a little money or to pay on her bill. But maybe Sally Arnold was really looking for awful things, Jenny imagined, like snakes and dead animals for cooking into magic spells. Jenny Fox stared hard as Sally Arnold passed the store.

On Tuesday Jenny hid behind the pine tree next to the store, waiting and watching for the old woman. Then down the mountain Sally came swinging a battered pail she must have found. Wild gray hair stuck out under her worn hat. "Can always use another pail," Sally cackled to herself.

"What does she want with that piece of junk?" wondered Jenny. "Probably for stirring up some magic," she decided.

On Wednesday Jenny stopped sweeping the store's porch, leaned against her broom, and watched a bluebird singing on the fencepost.

"A new broom sweeps clean."

Jenny jumped. "Who said that?"

"Looks like the one I found is done with cleaning, though." Old Sally Arnold walked by waving an old worn broom. "Little mama bird there is looking for a new home. She'll be laying eggs, having babies soon." Sally Arnold smiled.

And before Jenny could say a thing, Sally Arnold left. She poled herself along, using the old broom as a walking stick, the stub of straw in the air.

"Up close she looks real witchy, except her smile is sweet, not scary at all."

On Thursday Jenny watered the geraniums. She looked down the road. Sally Arnold again! The old woman had cut wild grapevines and wound them into circles, slipped her arms through, and lifted them onto each shoulder, little tendrils hanging all around. She bent forward as she walked and the vines made leafy wings over her like a ragged angel. Jenny offered a little wave as Sally passed.

Grandpa Fox's general store was the only one in Lynn Camp, where two mountain roads met and the creek made a big bend. Friday was hot, so that afternoon Jenny went down to the creek. She loved to sit on the bank, skip stones across, and watch the water move. She still wished she had a friend to play with her.

And then along the creek walked Sally Arnold! Jenny could tell that Sally had been to the mud flats because she was carrying reeds and cattails in her arms. Jenny saw that Sally Arnold wasn't much bigger than the gatherings she carried.

"Can't wait 'til I get these home," Sally said when she
saw Jenny.

Jenny thought Sally looked awful hot and tired, so she
helped carry the reeds and cattails up the bank, but only
to the fork of the road. Jenny still wasn't sure about Sally,
and she was too shy to go any farther.

Jenny watched old Sally Arnold walk away. "She wouldn't have hurt me or boiled me into a potion. Maybe she's just lonely," thought Jenny, who knew a little about being lonely, too.

On Saturday night Jenny was just filling Mr. Franklin's order when Sally Arnold walked into the store. After buying nails, hard candy, and tea, Sally Arnold brought out her harmonica and Grandpa brought out his banjo. Jenny got her fiddle and Sally taught her a new tune. Soon the store was full of smiling, dancing people. Later that night after talking, making music, and dancing, Sally said good night to everyone and walked home, humming the tune as she went. Jenny was sure no witchy woman could be such fun or make music like Sally Arnold.

On Sunday Jenny watched Sally walk home from the little white church, with a fan in one hand and a black book in the other. A long afternoon stretched before Jenny. The store was closed. Grandpa was napping. Nothing to do. No one around. Jenny wondered about Sally Arnold. What kind of old woman was she? Jenny set off up the hollow to locate Sally's place and to find out.

She neared Sally's cabin and hid in the bushes. The old woman sat on the porch just above the creek. Her cabin seemed held together with old tin signs and pieces of barn wood stuck every which way like a crazy quilt over the walls. Spying on Sally was fun, Jenny thought. Maybe now she could find out why Sally Arnold carried home all that junk. What did she do with it anyway?

But just at that instant, Jenny's foot slid in the soft mud. She started down the bank. Jenny grabbed a clump of grass to stop her fall. It pulled out. She grabbed onto a bush. It broke off in her hands. Jenny hit a groundhog hole, screamed, and landed face down in the creek. She couldn't breathe. She couldn't see. Jenny splashed like crazy. She got her feet under her and came up for air. Brushing wet hair out of her eyes, Jenny looked straight into blue eyes framed in wrinkles. Caught snooping by Sally Arnold!

"Well, look what the creek brought me today! Company!" laughed Sally Arnold. "You all right, Honey? Anything broken or scraped?" Sally plucked Jenny out of the creek and helped her up the bank to her cabin.

At first Jenny wanted to get as far away as fast as she could from Sally Arnold. Jenny was embarrassed to be caught while spying, and she was a little shy, too. But soon she felt safe and warm gathered in Sally's arms after her plunge in that cold creek.

Later Jenny sat on the porch swing with Sally. Scattered about were all the things she had seen the old woman carry. The battered pail held water, reeds, and cattails. Nails were driven into the four corners of boards. The broom handle was cut into short lengths and little vines were lashed onto the ends.

"What are you doing with this mess?" Jenny asked.

"Why, girl, I've been making gathering baskets. You ever made one?" Jenny shook her head no. "We'll take care of that!" said Sally.

Holding boards on their laps, they laid cattails between the nails. Jenny and Sally Arnold wove reed after reed through the cattails—over and under, over and under—and the baskets took shape, growing taller with each reed.

A fish jumped in the creek. Sally's old cat stretched and yawned. Hummingbirds visited the bright flowers beside the porch. Jenny and Sally talked. They sang a little, too.

Then Sally Arnold lashed pieces of broom handle in place to make the handles. Carefully, she pulled the reeds and cattails away from the nails. Lifted them from the boards. "Look here, girl!" Sally exclaimed. "Finished!" And there they were, two fine gathering baskets.

Sally Arnold walked Jenny home, each carrying her new
basket. Together they stood and watched the bluebird fly off
and return with a long piece of straw trailing behind her.

"She's making a bed for her family what's coming," said Sally.

Jenny held Sally's hand. "She gathers what she needs from
what she finds and makes something new."

Now whenever Grandpa doesn't need her help, Jenny
walks the roads or creeks with Sally. Each carries the basket
she made and together they search ditches and road banks.
They gather berries, flowers, and old bottles when they can
find them. Mushrooms, ginseng, and wild asparagus in
season. They talk. They sing. And they never, ever walk
down the road empty-handed.